THE LEGEND OF THE
CHRISTMAS ROSE

BY WILLIAM H. HOOKS

PAINTINGS BY RICHARD A. WILLIAMS

HARPERCOLLINSPUBLISHERS

Library of Congress Cataloging-in-Publication Data
Hooks, William H.
  The legend of the Christmas rose / by William H. Hooks ; illustrated by Richard A. Williams.
    p.   cm.
  Summary: The younger sister of the three shepherds secretly follows her brothers who are traveling to Bethlehem to see the Christ Child.
  ISBN 0-06-027102-7 — ISBN 0-06-027103-5 (lib. bdg.)
  1. Jesus Christ—Nativity—Juvenile fiction.   [1. Jesus Christ—Nativity—Fiction.   2. Christmas rose—Fiction.   3. Brothers and sisters—Fiction.]   I. Williams, Richard, 1950–   ill.   II. Title.
PZ7.H7664Ld   1998   98-45565
[E]—dc21   CIP
                                                                                                           AC

              1   2   3   4   5   6   7   8   9   10   ❖   First Edition

For

Maryellen Bowers,

who introduced me to *Helleborus niger*

—W.H.

In loving memory of

Ange Weisman

—R.W.

DOROTHY had three brothers, tall and strong,
shepherd giants who guarded their father's sheep.
At least they seemed like giants to her.
Dorothy was born late,
long after the youngest of her brothers
had gone to the fields to tend the flocks.
Her mother, who had given up hope
of ever having a daughter,
named her Dorothy, which means
"gift from God."

DOROTHY had three brothers, tall and strong,
shepherd giants who guarded their father's sheep.
At least they seemed like giants to her.
Dorothy was born late,
long after the youngest of her brothers
had gone to the fields to tend the flocks.
Her mother, who had given up hope
of ever having a daughter,
named her Dorothy, which means
"gift from God."

Now in her ninth year,
Dorothy was allowed to carry a goatskin
filled with fresh water to her brothers.
But they still treated her like a small child.
"Little Dot! Little Dot!" Joab would shout.
Then he would scoop her up, toss her high
into the air, and catch her in his arms.
Micah would twirl her around and around
until she was dizzy.
"I'm not a little Dot," she would gasp.
"I'm your biggest sister."
"And you're the youngest and oldest sister, too,"
teased Jonathan.

One day when Dorothy was bringing water
to the fields, she spied strangers on the road.
Quickly, she hid until they were out of sight.
Then she rushed to her brothers.
"Did you see the strangers?" she asked.
"Do you think they are robbers?"
Micah laughed and said, "No, they are not robbers."

"All week now we have seen
many people along the road," said Joab.
"The great Roman Emperor, Augustus,
has ordered that all must return
to the city of their birth to be taxed.
Father says we should stay in the fields
and watch over the sheep tonight,
with so many strangers abroad."
"Oh," said Dorothy,
"how I'd like to sleep under the stars!"
"Well, you can't, our biggest, littlest, oldest,
and youngest sister," said Jonathan.
"Off with you, Little Dot," said Micah.
"We'll see you tomorrow morning.
And we'll be hungry as bears."

Dorothy's mother called her early,
while the morning star still was shining.
"Wake up, sleepy one, and help your mother
with the breakfast bread."
They pounded the dough into flat, round cakes.
Dorothy took the first batch outside
to bake in the clay oven.

Suddenly, through the first pale glimmering of dawn,
Dorothy saw a man running and waving his arms.
Soon he was near enough for her to hear him plainly
and to see him clearly.
"Micah!" she called. "What is wrong?"
"We have seen a host of angels!" shouted Micah.
Fast on Micah's heels came Joab, crying out,
"Glory to God in the highest!"
And then Jonathan ran up, shouting,
"We heard singing in the skies!"

Dorothy's father rushed outside.

"My sons, what has come to pass?" he asked.

All three spoke at once.

Their father raised his hand.

"Keep silent," he ordered.

"Let my eldest son, Micah, speak."

"Father, last night,

while we were watching over our flocks,

an angel of the Lord appeared.

A strange light shone around us—"

"And Father," Jonathan broke in,

"we were sore afraid!"

"Silence!" his father ordered.

"Speak on, Micah."

"It's true we were frightened, Father,
but the angel told us not to be afraid.
'Fear not,' said the angel,
'I bring you good tidings of great joy,
which shall be to all people,
for unto you is born this day
in the city of David, a Savior,
which is Christ the Lord!'"

As Micah paused for breath,
Jonathan spoke up. "Father, the angel told us
we would find the babe in a manger
in the city of David."
"That would be Bethlehem," said their father.
"The prophets have foretold this."
"Father," said Micah, "allow us to go to Bethlehem."
"Yes, my sons, the Lord has made this
known to you, and you must go.
And you must take a prize lamb
to this newborn king."

It was more than a day's journey to Bethlehem.

They would arrive after nightfall.

Dorothy and her mother scurried about

packing food for the journey,

finding the three best cloaks

and the sturdiest sandals.

How Dorothy longed to go with her brothers.

But she dared not ask,

well knowing what the answer would be.

Sadly, she watched until they were out of sight.

The moment her brothers vanished,
Dorothy's feet began to move.
It seemed she had no control over them
as they sent her running after her brothers.
All day she followed from afar,
careful not to let them see her.
She never tired or minded the hot sun,
nor did she feel any hunger or thirst.
She must see this child
of whom the prophets had foretold.
As night drew on, Dorothy feared
she might lose sight of her brothers.
And soon a greater fear struck her heart—
she had no gift for the child.
"What can I bring the babe?" she cried.
"I have not even a coin to buy a pomegranate.
What can I bring to show my love?"
Ashamed to enter the city without a gift,
Dorothy hid behind a rock and wept.

Suddenly, she heard a rush of wings
beating in the night sky.
She gazed upward
and saw, in a burst of light,
an angel waving a flower of purest white.

Dorothy covered her face and waited
until the rush of wings faded away.
When she opened her eyes,
she beheld a wondrous sight.
All of the ground surrounding the rock
was carpeted with white flowers.

She filled her arms with the snowy blossoms,
and rushed to find her brothers.
They had vanished into the dark city.
But somehow her feet guided her
through the streets to the manger.
There lay the newborn babe,
surrounded by gifts of gold, gems,
frankincense, myrrh, and a prize lamb.
Richly adorned kings stood
with three sturdy shepherds, her brothers.

Awed by all this splendor,
and fearing her brothers' wrath,
Dorothy held back.
Finally, she gathered the courage
to approach the manger.
Timidly she bowed her head
and laid the flowers at the Christ child's feet.
To her amazement, the babe
turned away from the other gifts.
He smiled at Dorothy
and reached for a blossom.
He held it in his chubby hand.
A blush of the palest pink
infused the pure white flower.

Dorothy need not have feared
the wrath of her brothers.
They were filled with the spirit
of the Christ child and carried her safely home,
but not before she led them to the rock
where the miracle had occurred.
There she found a single rose
and carried it home with her.
Or, it should be told that Micah,
her giant of a brother,
carried a tired, sleepy little Dot
and her plant
most of the way home.

The plant grew and multiplied.
Dorothy used it to heal many illnesses.
She shared it with friends and strangers,
who came to learn of its power.
Today, Christmas roses grow
throughout the world.
They bloom at Christmastime—
even in the snow.

*T*HE CHRISTMAS ROSE, also known by its scientific name, *Helleborus niger*, has a long history of medicinal usage and has inspired a rich trove of myths and legends. The legend told here harks back to the birth of Christ, giving the plant its common name, Christmas rose; but there are also earlier legends stretching back many hundreds of years before then.

In Greek and Roman times the plant was revered by herbalists for its power to cure madness, nervous disorders, and heart ailments.

According to one Greek legend, the plant was first discovered by a poor shepherd around 900 B.C. The shepherd used it to cure his sick cattle, and later to heal his neighbors' nervous conditions. His fame spread, and the King of Argos sent for the shepherd to cure the madness of his three daughters, who suffered from the delusion that they had been changed into cows. The shepherd's cure was successful, and he was awarded the youngest daughter's hand in marriage.

During the Middle Ages, *Helleborus niger* continued to be used to treat madness and heart ailments. It also became popular with soothsayers and magicians. Sorcerers claimed that a powder made from the plant could make them invisible.

Modern chemical analyses reveal that the plant does contain three digitalis-like substances that have proved effective in the treatment of heart ailments.